GH00864184

Published By Two Sides To A Coin LTD

Copyright © Xavier. L. P 2015

All Rights Reserved

Disclaimer

This is a work of fiction. Names, characters,
businesses, places, events and incidents are
either the products of the author'?s imagination
or used in a fictitious manner. Any resemblance
to actual persons, living or dead, or actual events
is purely coincidental.

Special thanks

To my family in particularly my son and girlfriend
Love you guys. My brother, sister and mother
believing in me and my work.

To those who contributed to my Kickstarter
project, you kept me going despite the stops.

To those I may not have mentioned but who kept
me going whether good or bad.

And a special thanks to you the reader.

Many sleepless nights went into this project so
please enjoy.

Rest In Peace Uncle Rob & Granddad.

P.s This collection was inspired by the
gentrification of local estates and was made to
preserve our history .

Content Page

Introduction

The feeling of not being able to move or even worse being trapped by your status and area. It's easy to get caught within our environment a little incident can cause a grudge, the beginning of an evil thought process or an instant reaction which can lead to unfortunate events.

It would be easy to say find something you love and focus on it, but that's not always the case. So what are you doing for the time being? Don't be scared to make mistakes; just be conscious of the fact that you will have to take the wheel back one day. It may be a harsh road, and you may see things that remind you of where you should be, where you would like to be or even of where you use to be. However, the primary focus is to reach the point in which you want to be.

So you're trapped, asking yourself what you can do? Begin to find your creative voice keep it close to you; don't share it until you are ready, Its the most vulnerable art of self. With this same talent, you will one day show the/your world which you should look forward too.

These short stories are dedicated to those trapped within a concrete vessel. Be mindful of your thoughts and of your network.

Part of the bigger picture is to stay focused.

Neighborhood Hero

Avenue Press

July 3rd around 13:36 PM

The day flew by as it was washed away; with enough carbonated drinks to give them cramp. Everybody huddled in their groups, boys and girls, girls and boys, bickering and snickering amongst themselves.

Tainted air halted the football fanatics. Goal posts quietened down as everybody took notice of the new arrivals. Steady pulling out a blade sharp enough to skin a carcass and still not be blunt.

What were you saying?!" said the attacker as he paced towards Lawrence. Lawrence lifted his arm to prevent the knife entering his flesh; yet it still sliced his skin leaving a wound, lengthy and deep.

Each attacker laid way into his ribs and face. Tightening the hold around his neck, as he tried to gain leverage over the boys.

Blades came out, while bottles were smashed and crack over and over again in attempts to level the field. However, it was apparent their actions were in vain. With their tail between their legs, they scattered off, but not before looking back within the distance.

Lawrence held his bleeding wound in disbelief. It was a bloody victory! Murmuring crowds parted ways traumatized about his triumph, as Lawrence walked through the crowd without any chant of glory.

Local News

Temperatures burst during blazing heat
"Did you hear what happened?"

Unless they were there, it was all fabricated, persuading others of their truth. A watcher's idea of the event was sold thin to grant a stepping stone to excel their name.

Editor's Column

Suppressed emotions boil
"If that was me though."

Here we go again, replacing facts with fiction, this is the difference between reality and new age rap. Phony friends underestimate the value of friendship, the appreciation of hard work has dropped.

"That's why I always walk with my ting."

In a position of self-destruction. In a time when keeping it real was just a phrase. The ones that knew spoke their mind, even if they were branded a lunatic.

Readers letters

"Some moist yout."

The birth of enemies comes from your victories. People will talk about your losses, about your personal life never mentioning your good times, but that's not the worse part.

It's when you are mentally and physically unprepared; surrounded by people who wait for a silent attack, all they can do is separate. Silently passing signals that something is about to happen, only staying to witness your demise.

Simple Rivalry

First Leg

"Pass it."

"Switch it back, Switch it back."

Demonstrating early signs of composure, as the goal post rattles off its hinges. Burst open various drinks and ice poles. Pushing and shoving, pushing and thumping legs and bodies hold a beating. Determined to win by any means.

"Who's that."

"You trying to play footy you lot against us?"

"Sam, round up the boys."

Sweaty palms touch on arrival as everyone waits in anticipation. Ambitious young boys determined to win.

Boys that have never met share dreams of balling in their teens. Flip a couple of years faces encounter once more. Only now facial hairs are thick and spacious.

"I know that boy" muttering, as he brushed passed him.

A fragile figure, hidden within thick layers of clothing, as the withered like an old rag, as his soul wears his face.

"Didn't you use to play football?" said Sam

"Yeah" bursting through the crackled lips were his stained smile.

"Where are you going?"

"Training" Sam replied.

"What you play Pro? "

"Semi-Pro" Coughing away as cigarettes and weed consume his lungs "Send me your number if you ever want to give football another try."

Pulling out two phones

"Take this number," reluctant to answer the call on the phone.

"What's your name again, so I save your number?" said Sam palming the phone back.

"Save it under, Johnathan."

"Who are you?" pushing pass Johnathan was a meaning mugging group of boys.

Sam stood courageously, pressing his forehead against the boys. Before they knew it, they began to push and grab each other unsure of the next move.

"Where are you from?"

Sam looked up as to look for help from Johnathan. Unable to make eye contact through the thick crowd of young men.

"Should I jab him" before Sam knew his ribs had been trampled on like an afternoon rush hour. He looked up to finally make eye contact with Johnathan, fearfully looking on from a distance.

Everyone dispersed at the sounds of sirens "We got them back" said one of the boys.

"That was overdue" struggling to breathe and keep upright.

Johnathan's face fell towards his hands "that wasn't him" whimpering cowardly in his corner.

"How do you know?"

"I was cool with him a few years back"

"Doesn't bother me someone was getting rushed today regardless."

In retaliation, Sam's friend gathered a group of boys to take a look at the situation. Sam was younger than the rest of his friends. He had the most potential at football, so it was paramount for him to dedicate himself to a pro team.

Second Leg

"Your sick, what's your name?" Said Sam

"Johnathan"

"How old are you?"

"11. twelve next month."

Johnathan lifted his head. "I'm 14; You should jump on Pro Football."

Struggling to hold the smile within. Twisting and turning, as Sam tried to grab the other boys attention, hoping they heard the news.

"What do you have a phone?" Johnathan said pulling out the latest Nokia.

"No" Sam replied as he looked at Johnathan's phone.

"I will come back next week to bring you down to the training ground around 7 O clock".

"You have his number?" said Sam's friend.

"Yeah, why?"

"Just phone him and say you want to link up."

Sam's pale face stained by a black eye seemed to grow bigger the more his friend looked at it.

"Pass the phone."

Everyone grew silent anticipating the event. Some chose to entertain themselves by flirting with passing girls; while others would punch the wall to increase their adrenaline.

"This is Alex from the football management team; Sam passed us your number. I'm giving you a call to let you know we have tryouts coming up today if you can make it."

Text Message "Hi, Alex Sorry I missed your call. Can you send me the location please?" replied Johnathan

"Yes, will do."

It was all going too smooth for Sam's liking as gripped his stomach.

"I've got to go" everyone grew silent again as Sam's friend was typing away on the phone.

"Cool Johnathan should be here in twenty minutes."

"Listen, Sam; I'm not gonna lie you have to put in some work."

"I don't think that's necessary."

"Are you gonna be a coward all your life?"

"I just want to kickball."

"What good is that when people treat you like some dickhead."

"I don't care as long as I can play ball."

"Give me your phone."

"Why?"

Pushing his face as the group of boys held his arms.

"Give me that" pocketing his phone.

"You can bounce now." as Sam friend shooed him away.

"Narh, my phone Bro."

"What do you stand for?"

"Please"

"Answer me that, and you can have your phone."

"Just give me my phone please, Marcus."

Forcing his fist through Sam's body warmer as he left the punch to soak within his stomach.

"You should stand for something, or you will fall for nothing."

Sam waddled off as his heart continued to beat away.

"He's coming now," said one of the boys.

"What do you like, arsenal." Said Johnathan

"Better than, Tottenham" replied Sam

"Let me grab some of that water please."

"Don't backwash it."

Chuckling amongst themselves as everyone began to cool down from the day.

"I'll see you next week yeah."

"I'll be by the shop."

Clutched in hands were the fist of fury and tasteful belts of pain.

"Quiet I can seem him walking through the car park."

"Aha, grab him."

"Pussy, where are you trying to go?"

"LET ME GO"

Johnathan's blood sprayed everyone within his facility.

"Bang him in his blockhead."

They groped his hoody and then began to fist him in his ribs, legs, and spine. Pummelled by feet of all sizes.

The remaining attackers pulled back, as they continued their journey for the bitter taste of vengeance.

"Let's go."

Aggregate

Johnathan's fragile cry echoed across the field. Twisting and turning flattening the grass

"mum, dad"

Forcefully peaking at the figure that stood above him.

"Come, get up."

His limp body embraced what the wet pitch.

"I'm cold."

Resting him across his shoulders as they headed towards the car park.

"I don't know why you young guys carry on like a bunch of muppets."

"It's not like that coach."

"What is it like, Sam."

"Coming from a different area means you are coming from a different mindset."

"Fighting is a waste of bloody time."

"Two boys share the same dreams, yet coming from different areas means you cannot communicate and help each other."

"Unfortunately" Johnathan replied

Digits Game

"Are those your real eyes?"

My flirtation skills are little to none. Fake giggles
and real lies young men love it the most; racking
up points like we do this to boast. There isn't a
girl who passes by that's not a boomting.

Fly girls fly by on the bus. Crooked necks are
turning to see, playing it cool, playing it safe but
you won't see another face like her's again.

"You lot fall back!"

You have no rights. Don't cause a fight snuffing
your friends for a friendly time.

"Bring your friends to the endz, and we can meet
at morleys."

Smooching on a late night, you know its date
night and a couple of dead friends a scrape or
two nothing but nappy heads.

"I have two girls coming!"

Whose more thirsty for a Kirsty or more keen for

a Christine.

"I don't have any links."

Sob stories bring more than a purse out.

"Come then, but be quick though."

Snakes!

"I'll bring you in on the weekend" refuse to miss out on the big occasions you know five to six friends.

Bowling paid for, lunch paid for and borrowed clothes off an older sibling. Friends tend to lean on me to boost them up; like when their confidence is way-way low; therefore it's best to move alone. In hopes that training day has paid off.

"Good, evening ladies."

"Where are the two boys that were just with you? Why did they run off?"

"They were scared to approach you."

"What is your name?" Said the sexy friend.

"Spectre"

"So you're a road boy."

"I'm not familiar with the term."

I'm just precautious with my words. Like an onion, we as young men peel ourselves away for a special one. Unique individuals pass a week, talking becomes a routine.

"So what did you do today?"

Proceed with routine convo add a spice of life.

"I had work today, but Oh My God I had the weirdest day"

Settled in not as far as to say my mum knows your mum. However, we are comfortable in each other's homes.

"Let me hear one of your poems."

"Hmm"

"Let me just hear one please."

"Alright, It's not finished though so don't laugh."

Nothing is more refreshing than that first drink
Crooking my neck back
as I watch the stars duck and dive from the
clouds
Lighting and thunder transcend from the sky
while shells pour down to wash them away
Somehow I know they will be safe.

- Untitled

"Why don't you go to an Open Mic show?"

"Nah, I'm not that soft."

"You fool, you should definitely try it out! I think you will go far!"

Branded

"What was that noise?"

"I don't know."

She giggled, as she pulled him closer. Slowly placing, carefully positioned kisses. Both were young, both in love.

"Are you okay to go ahead?" he said

"Do you want to?" she giggled.

Not to seem too hasty he nodded and smiled, she smiled they continued.

End of summer period

"Hey"

"You alright."

No conflict, no regrets, no worries unless a friend knew; which would then mean a friend went to tell a friend. Well, let's just hope they are good friends.

"Did you two have SEX!" Blurted out Luke's friend

No privacy, no dignity, no remorse.

"...what? She replied

As her face sunk and silence reached her ears. Still, that couldn't block a loud crowd, from entering their presence.

"Errgh you two had sex," said Chantelle

"I heard you gave him head," said Estelle as they both giggled and bickered among themselves

"Yeah you look like the type" replied Chantelle.

"Errgh you hoe."

"Look at her with them worker boots" with a small trickle of piss; they burst out laughing.

"Pooh she smells like a wet dog."

Not a single teacher insight, not even the bell for

the class could save her.

Two years later

Still lingering on, still unsolved and look at who she is rolling with Rebecca, Danielle, Chloe. Outcast, from their previous social groups. Roaming around their town but well known throughout the borough.

"Yo, Rebecca" a group of boys shouted

"My size," said the boy seeking immediate attention, steady approaching the girls with confidence.

"Where are you lot going?"

"You alright, Michael," said Rebecca blushing yet still confident to approach.

Rebecca has whisked away with Michael; while the rest were soothed with warming words.

The boys looked unwell and poorly presented, none bathed, none cleansed; all reeked of

unwanted odors.

Swiped off their journey and led to an unknown house, everyone entered except her timid and out of place. Was she to go in or stay out? She was alone in an area, she wasn't too keen on, so with her friend she stayed.

Crowded with no more activities than a youth club. Closing her mouth, as she sat still as all her "friends" had gone. Surrounded by too many drugs and testosterone, she peeped an opening and took it.

"Where are you going?"

"anywhere but here" she whispered.

Instead, she cockblocked a friend, eager to please the needs of a fertile egg.

His friend popped in and produced a speckle of hope, no bigger than a chess piece.

"Ha"

Nonetheless, these were times of desperation.

"Grab it then."

"Ha, me?"

"Are you dumb!?"

She grabbed his bishop and tugged away, pushing him aside as he forced her face. She picked herself up, quickly ran out and stormed away.

Year 11

Caught by the whispering eyes as she got back into school. Followed by a flock of people with a barrage of questions.

"You went into Michael's house the other day," said Chantelle

"We know what goes on in there," said Estelle

"Your mother should be ashamed."

"What did you see me do?!" she replied

People looked back astonished by her voice.

"Bang her!"

Without hesitation, she threw a wild swing.

"Ooh"

"Did you see that?"

"That punch connected!"

"Estelle's bleeding!"

The teachers scurried over just in time "break it up!"

In the sheer shock of her retaliation, stunned her as she stood firm in place.

"Watch when I catch you after school," said Estelle holding her nose as the blood just gushed away.

Now the classroom howls of the incident. Only to encourage another round, like the last one wasn't bloody enough. She fought for something in the first round; the second round was for the sluggers.

Outnumbered, outgunned and outwitted, so many people were determined to see her fall. Still standing strong she fought for what she believed in. Leaving school with a cheerful five B gcses and a sprinkle of respect with her face battered & bruised.

A new start

College a sign of relief, a new start. A course you can get involved in. No friends not until you get your head straight.

"Hi, how are you doing."

"Fine, thank you."

Approaching this new relationship with such patience you either mess up now or later. A few months on still happy, still patient yet none the

wiser.

A few steps further on, she is reminded of turmoil. Two kids different dads and still single. She had never asked for this info; it was bestowed upon her.

Chantelle was now a struggling mother, with no one to help. She gave a short glimpse, before indulging in conversation. Chantelle looked back upon her still holding feelings while unwilling seeking sympathy.

A few years later

Still frowned upon, open heart, closed legs, eyes wide, yet her soul yearns for fulfillment.

Pushing him away, from on top of her.

"I cannot do this, Ryan."

"Why not?" he replied sexually frustrated.

"I changed my mind."

He continued to transform his words to smooth erotic persuasion, adjusting his body position. It soothed her soul, but she had made her mind up, what was she to do?

A month or two went by and then a few more. Sick, body weight still increasing and a baby kicking away no replies, and you even tried to e-mail. You've worked hard for what you need, and you're not letting anyone give you any No's.

No pity, No thank you.

24 Months Later

Dignity and the pride in which you hold your child and connect with them in your world. No one intervenes, no one believed yet you still succeeded.

But still, you have to wonder is it, love, you need.

"Hi, how are you doing" calm cool and collect

"What do you want?" or what can you provide?

"Would you like to go out on a date."

A new approach to your wounded soul, you've never had it like this before.

"Why not?" the soul replies

"I would love to but, my child would be home alone" she insisted.

It has been a few weeks in and your getting settled in. Visions intertwine, and you have no sign of any bad traits, but you have to wonder what lies in his mind.

"What do you think of me?"

Pass The Time

"Next customer please"

As each customers attitude and disrespect
slowly tear me away. I start to wonder how long
can I go on at this place? Knowing its not where I
choose to stay. My body aches from pain and
lack of sleep. But no pain no gain I suppose.

Service Is key!

You would think a customer saying "thank you" is
more awkward than a girl saying "fuck me
please" whilst balls deep. I'm giving the best
service I can; high pitched and cockney, Sir,
Madam.

"You have an hour lunch"

I choose to run and hide from this place rather
than considering to sit down and eat food. It isn't
as important as seeking a lovable distance
between me and this place. My face and your
face don't seem to match the policy of keeping a
smile on.

You choose the job you love; they love the job I

hate. Yet I seek a place where my presence shines brighter, rather than a foul essence.

"Excuse me, My shoes?"

"What shoes? You didn't ask me for shoes"

"Hi, Madam I've found your size" said a soft voice behind me

"You mistook him for me!"

Little to no eye contact this is the problem. The same ignorant person is probably the best friend of a police officer, quick to profile me.

"I have a complaint about these shoes"

I'll get the manager before you slap me in my face. Better yet know your place in this world. I finish in an hour wait outside and I will meet you there with that same mouldy face.

"Make sure you replen, clean and cash up before you leave!"

I burden my soul with an old folk tale; about how I need money for the finer things. Like a car, some trainers, new garments and fine dining. Not a penny to my name but every penny I gain, I go out to clear my mind and reboot for another days I don't look forward too.

Overtime

I consider it for a moment until I realised what my day would consist of impatient and rude customers. But I need the money!

"Oi you, neek. Party later you know"

"Juice & smoke"

"C'mon bro"

Emptying my pay check
from a ATM
as a crack fiend
politely asks for change

Sparing enough for a hamburger
hoping it will save her life

Failing to realise
shes still human
even as she taps her vein
her body cries out in pain

Consistent ads reassure my decision
Until finding the same lady down the alley
So how could my decision be in vain

Who would of thought such a thing
as if to say the cold aint cold
Like bellies don't cry
Never asking why shes in need of a high

Its mad to think soap cant wash away the sins
Unwashed hands smother
the faces of loved ones

So as my night begins as your night ends
pretend friends come around
over and over again
rubbing my back for assurance
wish me luck as I secure the performance
pull my clothes as if im not still in them

Mouths tickle for undesirable beverages

guzzling a large mixture of
Substances I ain't seen before
is this how she got here
lost and forgotten
amongst the twenty thousand people

vibzing
mellow
faded

I don't smoke but I'm still blazing
grips his lighter to show my appreciation

Buses quiet down
as lairy loud mouths disappear
She sleeps on me as I sleep on her ?

I can still taste the night
through burps of dysfunctional events

Soft long kisses
No need for a number
I'll call you a cab
she stares at me as I stare at her
Maybe I should tell a friend
to tell a friend The drugs ain't kicking in

keep it short
keep it brief
skip the small talk
lets just get to the point

- Circle Of Life

Cat On A Stoop

It almost feels like they need me, more than they need their fix. Whether it be small talk or life stories morning, noon or night I supply the ears.

Brown stained hands, piss yellow sweat marks with the faded patch.

"How you doing J."

Crispy notes unfold in my hand as we trade twice. Bills still rising, kids will stray, it's payday so down the pub you go. My phone still rings as the fill me in on a long day

I'll spend the time that you just worked for; nevertheless, I hope you stay high for you and yours.

"And then my manager Lily said you're late..."

Every five minutes its a story I hear.

"I just hate my baby father..."

Business is business.

A twenty minute sit down for the exclusive
clientele, embracing the vibe they bring.

This life's a delusion. Fragile relationships shape
the mold, you become heartless in time.

"My dad died today of cancer..."

My condolences

"Could I tick until Wednesday, it's just I have to
contribute to funeral costs."

let's be honest your only here because you owe
a dealer or two to make it worse you owe me
already

"You know I'm good for it..."

Simple matters could be solved but time
elongates such tasks one client could be the
reason for lack of funds

"I'll have the rest for you next week."

Now the tables have turned. The truth is this line

is a burden. Every day is Friday, get high and get by but its already in my stride a long lingering essence the guy, the lifesaver Mr. Socialite.

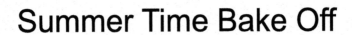

Summer Time Bake Off

Specs B - B - Q

Rubbing off joysticks, as sweat glands open up dispersing pungent scents unfriendly to the females.

Shoulder to shoulder lean on me brother, I advise you to suck your mum as a friendly gesture. Besides the graphics how can this game get any better?

Raising arms and pads "Offside? This game is fake!"

"Watch the formation now."

Every gamer is a pro manager, formation artist or player specialist.

"You gave me the shit pad."

Being sent to the shop for people you barely know.

"This is long" whisper the siblings of a party holder.

Snacking until the appropriate food is thoroughly cooked. Girls if not distant relatives then unrelated to the friends.

The early ones will get a look-in while the rest will have to wait. In fact "shout Shaun" he has a phone full of numbers for us to use, you know local fools for profit and gain.

"Where is the weed man?" family members show no remorse, blowing up a friend from about their younger days. Lights, camera, action start the show.

Keep the music, and the people to a minimum, gang rivalry call for victims as their day is dull and boring.

Good Evening, Warm Night.

"I heard Mark is on the estate, come we ride out," said Marcus unfazed by any of the functions taking place.

Faces so full it was hard to distinguish between the hunger and the taste of the food "Chill out."

Was it the females that gave him a strong sense of eagerness or was it the seeping desire to prove loyalty? "Don't come on your hype; just chill." said Specs guzzling nothing but Just Juice.

"Why are you putting on your jacket?"

"I'm going shop" like a child seeking a way out the house.

"I need more cognac.," said Marcus clutching his bottle.

"Slide my trainers, please."

"What you coming as well?"

"Yeah gonna head off home."

With a few surprise FIFA victories, it was only right to head off, as delaying my time would dampen my showboating.

"You lot chill! I don't want my house baited out" Said Specs.

"Why are you taking the pad?"

"Here you go," said Specs palming the pad over to me. "You beat me the first time, come give me a rematch."

"My girls at my house, I'll shout you tomorrow though"

"Say nothing sweet boy. Shout me later. If you see Marcus tell him not to bring back drama to my yard."

A lite Jog, and a few steps later.

"Yo, Marcus"

"Are you riding out as well YEAH?"

"Nah I'm cutting home, plus we don't need to go looking for trouble."

With a stern face, he looked around squinting his eyes as the streets light were blinding.

"Why you itching your balls bro."

"My blade init, you gonna roll then?"

"Nah, I'm looking my bed."

"Don't be a pussy!"

"Fuck it."

A few minutes in and I started to get butterflies, with crazy thoughts flicking through my mind.

Call me when you see this
 Message Sent to Elizabeth

"Why you on the phone?"

"Texting my girl."

"Don't start moving shook now."

"We haven't seen anyone for 15 minutes; I'm looking to cut."

"This is why I don't like you, some any pussyole yout."

"Both of you are moist," Mark said swinging his famous bike chain "Are you lot looking for us?"

Marcus froze, grabbed his hip and threw his knife away.

"What am I speaking to myself?"

We both silently stood, as I contemplated whether I could perform a quick hit and run.

"Come let's kick, Marcus" I nudged him twice and before I knew it, the same guy who was talking rubbish was frozen in position.

"Where is this party then?" said Mark

"What party!"

"So where is that music coming from?"

Marcus must have seen it when I wasn't looking at Mark and failed to remind me. All I remember is that by the time he reached the end of the road, I saw a big black gun.

"You banged me yeah...
 watch when I catch you."

We scattered across the road like ninjas. I was weaving through the cars. I jumped on Mr. Johnson's Car.

"Aha swear down," Specs said cackling over the phone.

"Marcus is moist anyway. I told you to stay and play FIFA."

"I had to go, my girl was calling"

"Still pussy whipped, Bro."

"Nah man shes calm. We were looking a holiday or Spa day soon."

"Its almost festival season and you're on lockdown. It's time for me to get some recruits"

"Ahahah! So you weren't kissing up my girls neck today. Moving real feminine giggling and all sorts."

"Obviously women like my soft side. I'm like one of them, makeup bears."

"Are you coming to bed?" as she so calmly caressed my head. To shoo her away would be to ruin the night. Placing a kiss on her neck and lips as my hand embraced her rosy cheek.

"warm the bed."

Twisting her body awkwardly to give me a fangirl smile. Winking back to send her away.

"Tomorrow, Specs"

"Late night smooching?"

"I'll shout you Tomorrow."

Stop & Search

"Where are you boys heading off to?"

Blocking our path as we walked, the officers perky as they stepped out their car.

With the arrival of two Bully vans, the officers started to get tight around the belt. Coming closer while, enforcing their intimidating presence.

"We've heard a large group of boys was causing trouble."

"You lads fit the description of some boys intimating the local neighbors."

Thoroughly checked before being rechecked, family relations only encourage the officers for a second check for their Re-assurance.

"We're not causing trouble here mate!"

"That's not the point we don't want you here," said the police.

A face of color but

ain't it funny how I blend in

embedded like
I just took a hit to the vein

foreign faces look
as if
all we do is complain

held accountable
for fathomed trouble

and to this day we learn

you could never embrace
my perspective

- Black, British & Young

Festive Season

Everybody meeting
Punani Greeting
Nobody wants you
with your pum pum cheesing

Chicken breast eating
Feds just grabbed him
Trust its a mad ting
But its festive season

- Festive Season

It was barely seven o clock in the morning, and he was prepping himself for the day. Picking out clothes borrowing his brother's cleanest pair of shoes.

We dressed accordingly, so there was no mistaking the agenda. Packing the essentials but not before using the razac. As a selected few gathered around chucking phones heated to concerning levels.

"I'm not looking to wait around any longer phone, Liam."

Prepared for war but going for fun. So we remain calm encouraging the clouds to unguard the sun we deserve.

Surrounded by loose girls and trouble, we realized the fruits it had brought us gods most beautiful hand picking of delights these scenes come but once a season festive season to be exact. So we will submerge ourselves until phones content.

And then it rained

We continued to grow as numbers pile up yet they never stepped to the beat or the rhythm of the tune.

"Who you watching."

Pay them no mind we will buck up in time. Gods greatest blessing burst through the clouds; holy rain swept away the decay of evil.

Tears run warm as my eyes burn.

We bubbled and skanked, champagne popped in

celebration all over his soft suedes, thank goodness for Crep Protect. Unfamiliar faces had never been to such events, scattered around to grab a feeling of the day. Slow hip movement on approach to the ladies, so they weren't new to this.

"What's good!?"

"What!?" replied Dan

"Show them we got the ting" faces once again not seen before in the commotion.

"Don't go over." Rebecca said as her soul held me.

Dan's reassurance came from numbers; numbers decline as evil thoughts come to mine. The crowd spread thin from twenty boys to forty watchers none of them familiar.

The blood, the screams, the distraught pleas covered in the bass and thumping speakers. Someone call his mum but shes more than a yell away. Such phone calls require special credit.

Striving to be good samaritans protecting their own lives. Now he lay flat hoping Jesus will save his life. Still, your mother warned you of this day.

"So you lot are just watching," said Luke looking down on a face once familiar.

I found a space to breath. Luke shook his feeble state and came to terms, and like them, gone within the thick crowd of sweat, confusion and continuous enjoyment.

Bus rides with headphones

Even the in-ear headphones couldn't keep out the voices rhetorical questions met with unfeasible answers. When I turn the volume down, I hear ghostly whispers.

Taking a glance out the window and asking could it be down to consumption. See we are all good guys at heart, but that's just an assumption.

With another two to raise mothers aren't proud. Lost in thought hoping she doesn't do this again. The world treats sons like we can be dismantled

and thrown away.

Two mothers cry, but the response is different
one met with hugs the other pushed to a
distance.

"Wrong place at the wrong time." but where
was he suppose to be?

Next Stop HMP

"Mum he was my friend."

Listing his Cons like damn what a shame. From
Assisting Pro footballers, a mentor and a close
friend or a savior at best

"He's a criminal."

Well damn how in vain.

Long Lost Friend

Aurora hadn't heard from her friend Delilah for awhile; even though days, weeks and sometimes even months would pass by before, she would get into contact. Nonetheless, she decided to stop by and visit her.

Usually, Delilah would jump out from behind her sending Aurora in a spook. On this occasion, however, she had felt a strong presence coming.

"Please, I need your help."

Said Delilah

"Why are you on your knees."

Aurora replied shocked at Delilah's feeble state.

"I've messed up this time, and I need your help, Aurora" Delilah pleaded.

Delilah was in a spiral of love, or so she believed. For if it were love, he would have been ruptured by the magnitude of affection. Such a pity, mind fucked before she was ever touched.

"Are you deluded, Delilah."

"He still loves me, I know he does" replied Delilah.

"He is a custom to a lifestyle fit for one, convinced he is successful" detested Aurora.

Aurora slowly became irritated about Delilah and Sam's idea of achievements, but still chose to listen.

"Why did he do that me?"

"Why did he do what?"

"My cousin threw it all away."

"Threw what away, Delilah?"

"Sam asked me to looked after some stuff; now he is looking for me."

"What stuff, Delilah?"

Her face dropped as if a part of her spirit left.

"I was holding drugs, and he wanted me to go up north."

Patting her box of cigarettes, as she pulled out her easy click lighter.

"I haven't spoken to my family."

"You have to come forward and tell them the truth," said Aurora as she went to comfort Delilah.

Delilah had got to involved to escape from what she had caused. Police had raided his place and found more drugs.

A narcissistic girlfriend, Blinded by her only delusion that she was here to assists in his journey.

"Could you make him see, I didn't mean it."

If only tears could cry

"I Just want him to see."

The hairs on her skin began to rise along with the summer breeze. Longing to be a young boy's reasons to want more from life.

If someone chose to become involved it was at their own risk of being disposed of; In spite of knowing this, she still aspired to gain acceptance of his essence.

It's possible she could have joined him on his quest for greatness. Guiding him away from temptation, however, it was this very thing that had brought her to his destination.

"Mmm, my smooth silk dress, his oaky aroma" triggered by her lust for luxurious lifestyles.

She appeared to smirk as Aurora looked at her in confusion. Her soul was slowly fading away her body frequency began to decrease dying as she lived on only to become a vessel.

Her corrupt mind had only given way to faults. She wanted it all and was driven insane by the same thing time will tell. How will her prayers be answered?

"I just want the life back; I didn't mean it."

First Times Your Last

Punch the clock

Date: 13/7/2014
Prison No: 3442356
Name: Nathaniel Oluba

Address:
45 cold harbour
Fortress drive
9ws 8qr

My Bro

"Just keeping my head up."

I hear you; it's still mad I didn't expect you to be in there. I don't think you did it arrogant as it seems it feels like a setup the way they described the case. Intelligence is a hard thing to trace.

Not too long for the sentencing, the judge neglected everything the police had to show maybe they don't have valid information but who am I to say.

"What's it saying out there."

Same old same old. You aren't missing anything the hood is the hood you know how it stays people going jail people coming out. I heard Yasmin has got a child as well.

I am not even on ends like that anymore; I'm out here! Heading up to Manchester for my boys birthday party its due to be live.

"Whats the girls saying, hook me up."

Lol, I'm speaking to someone at the moment we will see how that goes lol.

"HIT ME UP, VISIT MAN!"

Time to evaluate

"You remember that time?"

"How is your family?"

"Do you remember that girl?"

No matter how many questions you ask, they never show their weak side, but are we not family?

The weak pray on the weak. Damion was a good guy as well. I'm still shocked he has gone. Everyone would come to there own assumptions of constant blaming.

Gripping pads since the wire days now ninjas will call you bro from vast regions. You fail to see them reaching time and time again. So we destroy ourselves in time asking who can we trust.

"Don't watch nothing though I soon get a phone."

Landline on the landing

"My dad went to that boy's funeral the other day."

"Why?"

"That was my dad's godson."

915 Days on the clock

"When I touch road I'm moving differently."

The time you will never see back people see as paused moments of friendship.

Now I'm a family man and to see the look on your mothers face I want to help but do I have the time. Is it selfish to be with mine? Never lost in time, moving with the course of life.

No longer chasing the money like my younger days, too much time spent consumed within worthless resources.

Follow Your Own

Taking enough slow sips, that the alcohol would only tickle his throat.

"It was calm," Dre said looking across the room.

His eyes caught by excitement, sadness, and curiosity. Except one cutting through the false reality, the third eye in the room.

"I had a few girls messaging me and a couple of visits" swigging a mouthful of cranberry and vodka before continuing.

"It would have been nice to receive letters or some money to tide me over, but it's calm."

Bowing his head unable to see the reaction of those who sat in the room. A cluster of responses was only amounting to excuses.

Unaware that The third eye guest was still lurking, ears openly embracing the conversation.

He could sense the tension. He could feel the energy of those around. They weren't as loyal as they claimed to be. Using social media to

escalate themselves to a fickle level of expectancy.

Those who could afford to buy themselves into a life of deception broke they could hardly sense it.

"Did you meet anyone we know, Dre," said the amused pair looking for excitement.

"Yeah, I heard Shaq and Leon were in there running the wing."

Steadily holding the phones ready to take note and publicise what they had heard.

"Not all prisons are like that. I didn't even see them on the wing", Dre replied, as if he had been to every prison.

The phone calls, the visits, even down to the information he passed to his mother, he was alone in need of genuine friends and most importantly, admiration.

"My cousin said he saw you in there...", the curious one alert to the deception.

"Apparently, a couple of man in there were on to you.." sitting up as he continued.

Being In that particular prison, meant that a variety of people from all over were inside passing on information.

The room looked towards him pausing, listening, observing "Who's your cousin? " he replied.

Either way, it made no difference.

"Someone's phone is ringing."

"Yo... Yea I'm with him now. Is that what happened? Are you sure?" the third wheel still sat silently murmuring on the phone.

"I don't know what he would want to do, but I cannot speak right now so I will bell you back later, One."

The third wheel hung up only to catch a glimpse of the previous conversation.

"It's sorted," Dre said convinced that it would

divert the topic.

He sat back in his seat "What has been happening out here?"

Slowly trying to re-adjust to the normal gossip girls, who has got what and ways of getting it until he caught eyes with the third wheel.

"Come out the room, Ryan!" Dre declared. Ryan, his younger brother, picked up his belongings phone, charger, a cup of cognac mixed with pineapple juice leaving only a half-eaten plate of food and his well built untampered zoot and went.

Ryan just slowly starred as he left "Say nothing, Bro." The room continued to indulge in laughter.

As the day slowed down one by one people left the festivities. The smell of high grade exited along with the last few stragglers.

As the moon shone out with the stars, Dre lit his zoot pulling hard and exhaling slowly. Ryan came by his side calmly pulling out his zoot.

"You know I was told about what happened, Dre..."

Lighting his pre-rolled zoot before taking a slow deep pull "Why didn't you tell me?"

"You wouldn't understand, Ryan..."

"Let me see, Dre" insisting he shows him as his face sunk deep with compassion.

Dre pulled a drag on his zoot hard and began to cough. Ryan began to pat his back "Get the fuck off me, Ryan!"

Frustrated and still spurting out the inhaled smoke "You weren't there for me bro."

"I never knew, Dre" shallow tears filled his eyes as he began to drink the remaining alcohol.

"No one helped me they all left me to rot, even you, bro!"

"No, I.. I.. I.."

"Just cut, Ryan."

Depleted and in a hot fluster. Dre stood up and tried to regain his breath gazing at the stars before closing his eyes "I wish you were there. Why weren't you there?"

Ryan perched a seat beside him pulling again on the zoot.

"I always thought you didn't need me. I thought I was the one holding you back" Ryan said while blowing the excess smoke in the air.

"Reputation respect it's all so fickle these days anyone can have a piece."

"What you were saying prison made you a deep thinker, Dre" both chuckling as they shared a brief brotherly hug.

"Do you still wanna see?" Dre said stepping on the footstool ready to head back in. Ryan gave a slight nod and headed over into the front room.

Ryan distraught and in disbelief, scratched his head then rubbed his face. Slowly lifting his top Dre had revealed what had been left from a napalm attack his back appeared deformed and grotesque. Ryan's deflated soul could barely function.

"What is the plan, Dre?". Unruffled Dre held himself together looking aimlessly through the window.

"I don't know" he replied looking up and then down catching himself in the reflection of the mirror.

"We will see where the night takes us."

We Forgot To Enjoy The Sun

Bathed with rich thoughts
embedded in each cell

past ventures held in
containing joyous moments
of deprived times

confined minds let loose
to Rome and love

Visions deciphered
to their whines
dark; bittersweet
blood runs through veins and alleys

although what is seen is not felt
what is unspoken is undealt
a real connection will make the truth melt
merging two of the same

containing strength in every breath
and struggle in each step

Journal Entry No. 142

A heightened stage of violence, when corner

shops were capitalizing on bandanas for fun.

Tabloids were running around like children, printing false information like we grew up without manners. Nobody dreamed of being the worst; local areas tend to mad us.

Cleanse thy soul local stabbers turn to Christ; sins haunt your soul as you find it hard to sleep at night.

All this crime for a few pounds, to make it worse were incapable of saving a penny. Gas and electric, food, clothes, and travel, that's not to mention the personal expenses.

Why didn't I write about the nights, when the sun grew low while the heat burned slow.

It was not the dreams we dreamt, but the times we spent lost in what devoured our youth and train of thought. The many dead and buried, jailed and doomed, lost and confused.

Through dark times I pass by friends homes welcoming and warm. Little do they know I've

been through hard times, with even more reoccurring anxiety attacks.

Who would have thought that youth clubs would have saved us it amazed us that such people would help, adventures we took part in lost heroes consumed within their own lives.

Still Dreaming

While All this time we were enjoying the moment but rather than soaking up the rays we indulged in recklessness. Consumed within the suns boiling body, we let our minds burn out with frustration instead of picking a sweet spot in the shade.

Our thirst quenched with dry gin and yak. Vodka sweats beat down our glass, telling our stories of nights in the west end.

"What are your plans for Autumn?"

"Gonna head back to Uni," she said clasping my neck back.

"What you gonna do?" Why doesn't the sky have the answers? I lay my forehead upon hers as if a shot of an idea shall hit me.

"I'm gonna work."

"It's not too late."

"What for?"

"It isn't easy, being different."

"So what are you saying?"

"Maybe you don't have to go down that conventional route. You cannot escape who you are, but you can change who you want to be. Just take back the wheel."

Lightning Source UK Ltd.
Milton Keynes UK
UKOW04f1935281017
311789UK00001B/1/P